It's time for action.
COWS IN ACTION!

Genius cow Professor McMoo and
his trusty sidekicks, Pat and Bo,
are star agents of the C.I.A.
– short for COWS IN ACTION!
They travel through time, fighting
evil bulls from the future and
keeping history on the right track ...

Find out more at
www.cowsinaction.com

www.kidsatrandomhouse.co.uk

WORLD WAR MOO

Steve Cole

Illustrated by Woody Fox

RED FOX

WORLD WAR MOO
A RED FOX BOOK 978 1 862 30537 3

First published in Great Britain by Red Fox,
an imprint of Random House Children's Books
A Random House Group Company

This edition published 2008

3 5 7 9 10 8 6 4 2

Text copyright © Steve Cole, 2008
Illustrations copyright © Woody Fox, 2008

The right of Steve Cole to be identified as the author of this work has been
asserted in accordance with the Copyright, Designs and Patents Act 1988.

Set in Bembo Schoolbook

Red Fox Books are published by Random House Children's Books,
61–63 Uxbridge Road, London W5 5SA

www.kidsatrandomhouse.co.uk
www.rbooks.co.uk

Addresses for companies within
The Random House Group Limited can be found at:
www.randomhouse.co.uk/offices.htm

THE RANDOM HOUSE GROUP Limited Reg. No. 954009

A CIP catalogue record for this book is available from the British Library.

Printed in the UK by CPI Bookmarque, Croydon, CR0 4TD

*For my much missed grandad,
Dave Russell, whose tales of
World War II adventure I so enjoyed.*

★ THE C.I.A. FILES ★

Cows from the present —
Fighting in the past to protect the future . . .

In the year 2550, after thousands of years of being eaten and milked, cows finally live as equals with humans in their own country of Luckyburger. But a group of evil war-loving bulls — the Fed-up Bull Institute — is not satisfied.

Using time machines and deadly ter-moo-nator agents, the F.B.I. is trying to change Earth's history. These bulls plan to enslave all humans and put savage cows in charge of the planet. Their actions threaten to plunge all cowkind into cruel and cowardly chaos . . .

The C.I.A. was set up to stop them.

However, the best agents come not from 2550 — but from the present. From a time in the early 21st century, when the first clever cows began to appear. A time when a brainy bull named Angus McMoo invented the first time machine, little realizing he would soon become the F.B.I.'s number one enemy . . .

COWS OF COURAGE — TOP SECRET FILES

PROFESSOR ANGUS MCMOO

Security rating: Bravo Moo Zero
Stand-out features: Large white squares on coat, outstanding horns
Character: Scatterbrained, inventive, plucky and keen
Likes: Hot tea, history books, gadgets
Hates: Injustice, suffering, poor-quality tea bags
Ambition: To invent the electric sundial

LITTLE BO VINE

Security rating: For your cow pies only

Stand-out features: Luminous udder (colour varies)

Character: Tough, cheeky, ready-for-anything rebel

Likes: Fashion, chewing gum, self-defence classes

Hates: Bessie Barmer; the farmer's wife

Ambition: To run her own martial arts club for farmyard animals

PAT VINE

Security rating: Licence to fill (stomach with grass)

Stand-out features: Zigzags on coat

Character: Brave, loyal and practical

Likes: Solving problems, anything Professor McMoo does

Hates: Flies not easily swished by his tail

Ambition: To find a five-leaf clover – and to survive his dangerous missions!

Prof. McMoo's TIMELINE OF NOTABLE HISTORICAL EVENTS

4.6 billion years BC
PLANET EARTH FORMS
(good job too)

13.7 billion years BC
BIG BANG – UNIVERSE BEGINS
(and first tea atoms created)

23 million years BC
FIRST COWS APPEAR

(23 million is my lucky number!)

1700 BC
SHEN NUNG MAKES FIRST CUP OF TEA
(what a hero!)

7000 BC
FIRST CATTLE KEPT ON FARMS
(Not a great year for cows)

1901 AD
QUEEN VICTORIA DIES
(she was not a-moo-sed)

(by an Egyptian geezer)

2550 BC
GREAT PYRAMID BUILT AT GIZA

31 BC
ROMAN EMPIRE FOUNDED

(Roam-Moo empire founded by a cow but no one remembers that)

1509 AD
HENRY VIII COMES TO THE THRONE

(and probably squashes it)

1066 AD
BATTLE OF HASTINGS

(but what about the Cattle of Hastings?)

1620 AD
ENGLISH PILGRIMS SETTLE IN AMERICA

(bringing with them the first cows to moo in an American accent)

1939 AD
WORLD WAR TWO BEGINS

(or World War Moo as it is known to cows)

2007 AD
I INVENT A TIME MACHINE!!!

2500 AD
COW NATION OF LUCKYBURGER FOUNDED

(HOORAY!)

(about time!)

2550 AD
COWS IN ACTION RECRUIT PROFESSOR McMOO, PAT AND BO

(and now the fun REALLY starts...)

1903 AD
FIRST TEABAGS INVENTED

WORLD WAR MOO

Chapter One

OFF TO WAR!

The two fighter planes circled in the sky like birds of prey. The drone of heavy engines filled the air. Then the sharp sound of gunfire rattled out. One of the planes dipped sharply to dodge the bullets ...

"What an awesome show!" cried Pat Vine, a young bullock with white zigzags on his brown coat. Most of the time, Farmer Barmer's farmyard was a quiet and sleepy place – but not when the air show was in town, with stunt planes flying overhead! Pat lay down in the field with his hooves behind his head, enjoying the aerial acrobatics.

"These displays are brilliant, aren't they, Bo?"

"Hmm, not bad, I suppose," said Little Bo Vine, who was Pat's older sister. She was sitting beside him, blowing a big gum bubble. "It would be better if the planes fired laser beams and played really cool loud music on their stereos . . ."

Pat rolled his eyes. "Those are two planes from the Second World War! They didn't have lasers and stereos back in the 1940s."

"Boring!" said Bo.

Pat sighed. Bo was a rebellious milk-cow who loved fighting, fashion and painting her udder strange colours. Today she had decorated it with a Union Jack.

"You'd better not let anyone see that," Pat warned her. "They might work out that you are not an ordinary cow."

"They'll work out that *you* aren't if they catch you lounging on your back like that," Bo retorted.

"Exactly!" boomed a familiar voice from behind them. "So get up quickly, both of you!"

"Professor McMoo!" Pat beamed, jumping up onto all fours at once. He turned to greet McMoo, his greatest friend – only to find the professor standing on his hind legs with his hands on his hips, looking up at the stunt planes. "Hey, there's a Messerschmitt 109 fighting a Hurricane!" said McMoo. "*Fantastic!* Wonderful flying machines, first built in the 1930s, you know . . ."

McMoo was a large red bull with white squares on his coat and a twinkle in his eyes. Like Pat and Bo, he belonged to a very rare breed of brainy cattle – but the professor was the cleverest of all of them by far. The three big loves of his life were learning about history, inventing incredible gadgets and drinking tea. Sometimes he tried to do all three at once, but that got a bit messy.

"Professor!" Bo hissed at him, getting onto all fours like Pat. "Act like a proper bull, then. Here comes Bessie Barmer . . ."

In a moment, McMoo was grazing innocently on the grass. Pat did the same as Bessie came charging out of the farmhouse in an old stained nightgown. Even the sight of her made Pat's knees want to knock! Bessie was the farmer's wife, enormously nasty and fiercely fat. She hated all the farm animals. In fact, she hated most things – including aeroplanes, it seemed.

"Clear off!" she yelled, shaking her fist at the sky. "You noisy, smoky, silly

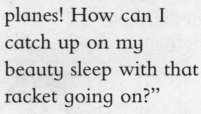

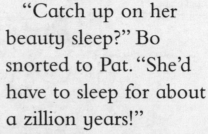

planes! How can I catch up on my beauty sleep with that racket going on?"

"Catch up on her beauty sleep?" Bo snorted to Pat. "She'd have to sleep for about a zillion years!"

"My grandmother was a war hero!" Bessie bellowed. "If she were here now she'd sort you out. You hear?" But the planes kept on zooming noisily through the sky, and in the end Bessie stomped off back inside.

"Good riddance!" yelled Bo as she jumped up and blew a raspberry. "Miserable spoilsport."

Pat nodded. "Those planes *are* a bit noisy though. Bet they're a squeeze to get into as well." He smiled at McMoo. "I think I prefer to travel by shed!"

McMoo grinned. "Me too. How about a quick trip right now?"

Pushing past the pair of them, Bo zoomed across the field to the wooden doors. "Last one there sucks a thistle!"

"*First* one there puts the kettle on!" McMoo called back. And as the planes droned on overhead, he and Pat ran after her.

Most cows, no matter how extraordinary, would find it difficult to travel in a shed. But McMoo had secretly turned his humdrum hay-barn home into a marvellous, magnificent mega-machine. Using his brains, brawn and bits of old techno-junk thrown away by the scientist who lived next door, he had turned his cow shed into a *Time* Shed!

The professor's plan had been to leave the farm with Pat and Bo and go tripping through time. Why settle for reading about history when you could *live* it? But before they could go anywhere – or any*when* – they had been visited by mysterious cows from the far future . . . Cows who revealed it was Pat, Bo and McMoo's destiny to become top agents for the C.I.A. – the Cows in Action! This crack squad of time-travelling cow commandoes from the twenty-sixth century needed McMoo's genius to help them fight the F.B.I. – the Fed-up Bull Institute, enemies of free cows and human beings in all times and places . . .

No sooner had Pat and the professor followed Bo inside the shed than a loud alarm went off.

Pat gulped. "Is that the C.I.A. now, Professor?"

"Yes!" cried McMoo, kicking aside

a bale of hay to reveal a big bronze
lever. "And it sounds like a blue-cheese
alert."

"A blue-cheese alert?" Bo frowned.
"What's that?"

"It's one step worse than a red alert
and a whole lot smellier," McMoo
explained. "We'd better find out what's
happening!"

He pulled on the lever, and at once a
grinding, clanking noise started up. The
bare wooden walls flipped round to

reveal sophisticated controls. A large TV screen swung down from the rafters, trailing tangled wires and cables, while a huge, horseshoe-shaped bank of controls rose up from the middle of the muddy floor. Hay flew through the air as a large, battered wardrobe burst into view, crammed full of cow-sized costumes for every occasion in history. In just a few seconds, the grotty shed had become a super-advanced time machine (with fitting room included). The alarm stopped beeping as the image of a burly black bull in dark glasses and a blue sash appeared on the TV screen . . .

"It's yummy Yak!" cried Bo. "Director of the C.I.A.!"

"Hey, team," said Yak gruffly. "How's it going?"

"Not well," said McMoo. "I haven't had a cup of tea all day!"

"Bo forgot to put the kettle on," said Pat.

Bo grinned cheekily. "I didn't think it would suit me!"

"This is no time for jokes," said Yak gravely.

"Especially not jokes as old as *that* one," said McMoo. "The electric kettle was invented in 1922, and that joke was invented three seconds later! Then, when the automatic 'stop-boiling' version was invented in 1930—"

"Er, Professor?" said Pat, pulling some hidden tea bags from a pile of straw. "Perhaps we should hear what Yak has to say?"

"Thank you, Pat," growled Yak wearily.

"As you know, a blue-cheese alert is super-serious. The F.B.I. has been causing us lots of problems lately, stealing huge amounts of butter."

"Butter?" McMoo frowned. "I always knew they were slippery customers, but even so . . ."

"We think they are trying to keep us busy while they commit a big time crime," Yak went on. "As always, they want to change history by getting rid of humans and putting killer cows in charge of the planet."

Bo blew another gum bubble. "But the question is, how will they try it this time?"

"That's what you must find out," Yak told them. "We have traced them to the year 1940."

Pat gasped. "The Second World War was happening back then!"

"You know it, trooper," said Yak gravely. "And while we try to stop their butter-burgling, you three must pop back to the past and stop *them*!" He paused. "We have just discovered that three ter-moo-nators have been sent to 1940 already."

"*Three?*" Pat gulped. Ter-moo-nators were the F.B.I.'s deadliest agents – half-bull, half-robot, and sneaky and sly from their horns to their hooves.

"Don't worry, bruv," said Bo cockily. "I'll smash their metal snouts in, however many there are!"

"I am beaming over co-ordinates for the last location visited by the F.B.I. in that time," said Yak. Red lights flashed on the main bank of controls as the Time Shed's computer received the data. "I am also sending you some things you may find useful in that time."

McMoo looked hopeful. "Any tea bags included?"

"No," said Yak firmly as a small pile of papers appeared in a flash at the professor's feet. "Now, get going, gang . . . and good luck!"

The screen went dark.

Pat passed a cup of tea to Bo and a bucket of the stuff to McMoo. "Looks like we're going off to war," he said nervously.

"Indeed we are," murmured McMoo. "To one of the biggest and deadliest wars in the whole of human history . . ." He drained his tea, chucked away the bucket and yanked on the take-off lever. "It seems that this might be our most dangerous mission yet!"

Chapter Two

BLITZ AND PIECES

The Time Shed clanged and shook and hissed and rattled as it hurtled back through time. Soon, with an enormous *CLONK!* it landed in a dark, deserted yard behind a line of moonlit houses. Pat felt a tingle of excitement in all four parts of his stomach.

"London, on the evening of September 13th, 1940," McMoo declared, checking the destination meter. "We have arrived during the Blitz."

"What's the Blitz?" asked Bo. "Who's fighting who in this war, anyway?"

McMoo turned to the TV screen. "Computer, give us the Second World War file."

++World War Two. ++Began 3 September 1939. ++Nazi Germany, led by Adolf Hitler, invaded Poland. ++As a result, Britain declared war. ++Britain and the Allies (including France and later America and Russia) battled the Nazis and later the Axis powers (including Italy and Japan) on land, sea and air. ++Conflict in Europe ended 7 May 1945 when the Nazis gave up. ++Phew!

"Over five years of full-on fighting!" Bo gasped. "That's amazing."

"It's terrible," McMoo corrected her sadly. "Computer, give us some Blitz bits!"

++The Blitz was a series of Nazi bombing raids on cities in Britain from 7 September 1940—10 May 1941. ++Over 1 million houses were blown up. ++London was bombed for 73 nights in a row. ++Even Buckingham Palace was hit!

"Not a very friendly time to land, is it?" said Pat nervously.

"Good!" Bo declared. "And while we're waiting for a fight, I'll find us some 1940s gear so we fit right in." She charged into the costume cupboard, tossed a pile of clothes across the shed at Pat and the professor, then got changed

herself. "Oh, no! Is this all you've got?"
She came out wearing wrinkly
stockings, a brown wool dress with neat
little collar and
a string of white
pearls. "How
frumpy. And
these flat shoes
are rubbish!
Can't I wear
high heels?"

"Sorry, Bo,"
said McMoo,
struggling into
his suit. "The
government of
1940 is asking
all women to
choose flat-
heeled shoes
because high heels use wood – wood
that can be better used making planes
and weapons to help fight the war."

"*Wooden* you know it," said Pat with a smile. "Unlucky, sis!"

"Lots of other things are being conserved too, like food and clothes," McMoo went on, warming to his subject. "They're harder to get hold of when a war is on, and people might run out."

"It's called rationing, isn't it, Professor?" said Pat brightly, and McMoo nodded.

"You're such a geeky know-all, Pat," Bo complained.

"I wish you could ration your dumbness!" Pat shot back.

"Shut up, you two, and stick in your ringblenders," said McMoo, stepping between them. The shiny metal nose rings were useful C.I.A. inventions that tricked human eyes into thinking the cows who wore them were actually people. They also translated cow-speak into any language in any time.

However, other cows would see through the disguise immediately – and so too would any ter-moo-nators . . .

They all put on their ringblenders and looked in the special mirror that showed how humans would see them. Bo appeared to be a sensible young lady. Pat could be mistaken for a schoolboy in a white shirt and a grey blazer with long shorts tucked into his socks. And McMoo looked like a big businessman in a dark suit, bow-tie and bowler hat.

"Now, let's see what's out there!" said McMoo, his eyes alight with excitement as he charged over to the doors.

Outside all was quiet. Until McMoo slipped on his first step and found himself tumbling down a miniature mountain of bricks. "Whoops!" he yelled, rolling over and over until he landed with a noisy *CRUMP* at the bottom.

"Professor!" gasped Pat. In a moment, he and Bo were skidding and sliding down the steep brick-pile to reach him. "Are you OK?"

"Just about," he said, dusting off his clothes. "Welcome to 1940!"

"We've landed in a rubbish dump," said Bo, unimpressed.

McMoo shook his head. "This was once a row of houses. Now it's rubble. Bombs did this."

Suddenly, a strange, lonely wail started up, rising and falling like the howl of some enormous creature. Pat was gripped with fear. "What's that?"

"An air-raid siren," said McMoo grimly. "They were set off to warn people that bombers were on the way." Even as he spoke, the skies were filling with the noisy throb of powerful aircraft engines. "We must find shelter. Back to the Time Shed, quick!"

The cows tried to scramble up the pile of bricks. But it was no good – the loose stones kept slipping beneath their hooves and they fell back down. And all the time, the sound of engines grew closer . . .

"We must find somewhere else," McMoo yelled.

Pat peered into the gloom. "Hey, look, in the next street. There's a cellar outside that pub."

"Well spotted, Pat!" McMoo led the stampede towards it as a sinister whistling sound started up, falling in pitch the louder it got.

"I don't think much of that tune," Bo
panted.

"It's the sound of falling bombs!"
shouted McMoo. "Run for your lives!"

The next moment, there was a
deafening bang behind them, and a
huge fireball lit up the crumbling street.
Windows shattered and bricks flew
through the air.

"Get behind me!" Bo's sturdy hooves
were a blur of kung-fu moves as she
punched and kicked lumps of wreckage
away from them. But within a second,
the dreadful whistling had started up
again.

"Here comes another!" Pat cried,

yanking open the trap door in the pavement that led to the pub cellar.

"Get inside, both of you!" ordered McMoo.

Bo and Pat dived into the dark cellar and McMoo jumped in after them. Split-seconds later the sky was lit white by an enormous explosion. The ground shook as the noise of the blast boomed through the cellar . . .

And then, suddenly, a man fell out of the sky and flopped through the cellar doors. He landed right in Bo's arms! "Professor — are those planes dropping men as well as bombs?"

"The explosion must have knocked him off his feet in the street and into here," said McMoo,

peering at the man, who was panting hard in the pale moonlight. "Hello, old chap! Are you all right?"

Suddenly, a bright torch beam stabbed down from above. Pat shielded his eyes from the glare, looked up – and found a dozen soldiers pointing their guns into the cellar. They were aiming at Bo and the man in her arms – and at Pat and the professor too.

"Hands up!" barked one of the soldiers. "I'm Captain Walker, and you're all in big trouble. That man you're holding is a Nazi spy we've been chasing for some time!"

"What?" Bo dropped the man in surprise. "How were we to know?"

"Obviously *you* were trying to help him escape." Walker sneered at them. "Get out of there, traitors – you're all under arrest!"

Chapter Three

THE SPY'S SECRET

The soldiers marched the C.I.A. agents and the Nazi spy through the dark streets at gunpoint. In the distance, Pat could hear the clanging alarm of fire engines racing by. Flames were licking the rooftops, giving a red glow to the black night sky.

"How are we going to get out of this one, Professor?" he whispered.

"We aren't, Pat, not just yet," said McMoo quietly. "We landed in the last place the F.B.I. visited, remember? And straight away we've found a spy."

"Of course," Pat breathed. "The spy could be working for the F.B.I.!"

Soon the prisoners found themselves
herded towards a large, grand building
with white pillars outside. It looked like
a fancy hotel, but armed soldiers stood
at the doors. Once inside, the prisoners
were marched through an empty room
and down a long, winding staircase. It
took them a few minutes to reach the
bottom, and Pat's legs trembled at the
thought of what might happen to them
down here . . . Would they be tortured to
find out what they knew? Would they
be kept here for ever and never see
daylight again?

Captain Walker gave a special knock

on the door at the bottom of the staircase, and it opened onto a vast, busy room filled with people working at desks or talking on funny telephones.

"A war office," cried McMoo, gazing around in excitement. "Hidden underground, so the bombs can't get it. Imagine that!"

"There's a big weapons-testing centre too," said Walker. "This is one massive secret base, and I'm in charge."

"If it's so secret, how come you're letting us see it?" said Bo sourly.

"Because it's also got a prison," said Walker with a nasty smile, herding them towards a heavy iron door in one wall. "And *that's* where you'll be staying for the rest of the war."

Pat gulped as the door swung open to reveal a private office. Inside, a massive old man in a crumpled three-piece suit sat behind a desk. His grave, lined face seemed part bulldog, part bullfrog, but his eyes gleamed with intelligence.

"Oh, wow!" McMoo was pointing at the old man in astonished delight. "It's the British prime minister! Pat, Bo, this is *Winston Churchill*! One of the most important leaders of the modern world, and we're meeting him in person. Imagine that!" He laughed loudly. "I *love* time travel, I just love it!"

A heavy silence followed McMoo's outburst. Pat and Bo cringed.

"You are accused of a most serious crime, sir," said Churchill, his voice deep and gruff. "This is no time for playing the fool."

"You're right there – but wrong about us." McMoo reached into his pocket and pulled out the papers Yak had sent over to the Time Shed. He passed them to Churchill. "As you can see, my two friends and I are special super-secret agents working for King George himself. Far from helping this spy, we were actually *catching* him!"

Bo frowned. "We were?" she said, puzzled, and Pat gave her a little kick. "I mean, yeah! Of course we were."

"It seems you have top-level clearance," murmured Churchill. He looked at Captain Walker and nodded. "These papers are signed by the king himself. I'd know his signature anywhere!"

McMoo winked at his friends. "But he *wouldn't* know that it's been cleverly forged by Yak in the year 2550!"

"Professor, Pat, Bo . . . please accept my apologies," said Churchill. "And my thanks for capturing this dangerous man. We know he is a spy – but he refuses to tell us why his Nazi masters sent him here."

"I will never talk!" the spy declared. "*Never!*"

"I'll get the truth out of him," said Bo, rolling up her sleeves. "Hey, Pat – remember when you hid my earring and wouldn't tell me where? I got the truth out of *you*, didn't I?"

Pat gulped. "Well, yes, but . . . it took me *days* to recover."

"I will never talk," the spy repeated. But he sounded a little less certain now. "Er . . . never?"

"We have ways of *moo*-king you talk," said Bo. Then, suddenly, she pounced on the spy – and began to tickle him all over! Her hard hooves dug into his ribs and jiggled in his armpits and niggled at his knees. At the same time, her udder tickled his tummy.

"Noooooo!" The Nazi fell about, laughing so hard he was crying and aching and very nearly wetting himself. "Please, no more!"

"Tell us why you're here," said Bo sternly, tickling him with her tail. "Now."

"All right, yes! I will!" wailed the hysterical prisoner.

"Good," said Bo. She jumped off him and winked at Winston Churchill. "Easy when you know how!"

Churchill smiled. "Never in the field of human conflict have I seen such a thing!"

"Now, then . . ." McMoo looked down at the red-faced spy. "Start talking!"

"Very well," the spy replied. "I came here to kidnap the most brilliant scientist in this country. And I did it too."

"You did not," scoffed McMoo. "I'm still here!"

"He means the most brilliant scientist in 1940, Professor!" hissed Pat.

"Oh." McMoo frowned. "Who's that then?"

"Sir Ivor Throbswitch." Churchill looked worried. "He has been inventing special new weapons here in this very building. But I thought he was away on holiday . . ."

"I conked him on the head, dragged

him away and bundled him onto a boat," said the spy smugly. "Even now, Sir Ivor is being forced to work for us in a special laboratory in France."

"Why not send him to Germany with all your other scientists?" asked McMoo.

"My masters wanted him in France and they know best," said the spy firmly. "There he will make amazing weapons for the Nazis — so we will win the war."

"Never!" snarled Churchill. "Because as it happens, we have got *your* most brilliant scientist."

The spy gasped. "Not Doctor Von Gonk!"

Churchill nodded. "He sent us a secret message saying he wanted to come over to our side. Our spies have already smuggled him from Germany to France, where he is being guarded by my most trusted agent. Soon, Doctor Von Gonk shall be sent to Britain — to help us win the war . . ."

"That's not fair," said the spy huffily. "We had the idea first!"

"Tough," growled Churchill. "Captain Walker, remove this man and guard him well."

Walker saluted, and he and his troops marched the spy from the room.

"McMoo, we must rescue Sir Ivor before he can make weapons for the Nazis," growled Churchill. "And we must help our French allies deliver Doctor Von Gonk to us as soon as possible."

"You can send a group of super-secret agents over to France to sort things out," suggested McMoo. "Namely, us!"

Pat gulped. "Us?"

"Cool!" cheered Bo.

"Just as soon as we've had a quick cup of tea, of course," the professor added.

"I had the same idea myself," said Churchill, lifting a telephone and speaking into it. "Gloria, kindly make the tea – in our finest cups . . ."

"Are you sure about this mission, Professor?" Pat whispered.

McMoo nodded and lowered his voice. "The Nazis keep their top scientists in Germany, not France. I think it's the *ter-moo-nators* who have got hold of Sir Ivor. We *must* find out what they're up to . . . the future of the whole world could be at stake!"

Chapter Four

A FAMILIAR FACE IN FRANCE

Just a few hours later, McMoo, Pat and Bo were sitting together on a large plane, flying through the night over France with parachutes strapped to their backs. Captain Walker sat beside the pilot with a map, working out the best place to jump.

Pat's stomach was buzzing with nerves. "I thought France was Britain's friend in the war," he said, checking his parachute for the hundredth time. "How come the Nazis are there?"

"Hitler's forces invaded France three months ago," the professor explained. "But many people living there are secretly fighting back as part of the French Resistance – and helping the British too."

"Gotcha," said Bo. "So the French Resistance are looking after Doctor Von Gonk until they can send him to Britain."

"Right." McMoo nodded. "But with the Nazis controlling all ports and airports, getting him across the English Channel is incredibly dangerous."

Pat gulped. "How are *we* going to get back to Britain?"

McMoo grinned. "Carefully!"

Captain Walker came through to join

them and opened the exit hatch. Cold air rushed into the plane. "Get ready to jump, chaps – and er, lady-chap. If all goes well you should land beside a big wood, and a woman called Odette will take you to safety."

"See you down there, guys!" Bo hurled herself out of the plane. "Geronimooo!"

Pat took a deep breath and jumped after her. Suddenly, he was hurtling through the sky at 120 miles per hour! It was an incredible feeling. "Watch out, world," he cried. "Flying cow alert!"

After a few seconds he pulled open his parachute and floated down to earth. Everything seemed calm and peaceful – until he landed on Bo's tummy!

"*M-ooof!*" she gasped, scrambling up. "Watch your hooves, bruv!"

McMoo made a perfect landing beside them. Pat listened to the sound of engines growing fainter as Captain Walker's plane flew back home –

leaving them alone in a dangerous land.
He gulped. The thought was scary, but
at the same time amazingly exciting!

"Quick, this way!" hissed a French
voice from behind a nearby bush. "I
am the Resistance leader sent to greet
you . . . Odette LaBarmer!"

The French woman jumped up from

behind the
bush – and
Pat and Bo
gasped with
dismay. She
looked
exactly like
Bessie
Barmer!

"Oh, no!"
Bo wailed.
"We run

into Bessie's relatives wherever we go!"

Pat nodded. "And they're always
horrid."

"Shhhh!" McMoo warned them. "There may be Nazi patrols close by."

"What is wrong?" Odette looked a bit upset. "Why do you scowl at me? I bring you fresh baps!" She pulled out some bread rolls from her skirt pocket. "See?"

"They probably taste like poo," said Bo rudely.

"Quiet, Bo," McMoo said sternly, gratefully taking one of the offered baps. "You are supposed to be a *secret* agent, not a toxic one! Churchill said Odette was to be trusted. We must give her a chance."

"I suppose we don't have much choice, all alone out here," said Pat.

McMoo smiled at Odette. "Forgive my young friends, *madame*. They are tired and weary. And if they're anything like me they could do with a cup of tea!"

"Of course, *monsieur*," said Odette. "I have a little at my bakery. Come! We must move quickly . . ."

As she crashed away through the forest with McMoo close behind, Pat and Bo looked at each other.

"What was that funny thing on Odette's face?" asked Bo.

"I–I think . . . it was a smile!" Pat watched the woman wobble away in wonder. "Maybe *this* Barmer's not so bad after all."

"Maybe," said Bo, as they set off after the others. "But I think we should keep a very close eye on Madame LaBarmer, Pat. A very close eye indeed!"

After thirty minutes trailing Odette through the undergrowth, the cows reached a big bakery. The air was filled with the roar of fighter planes heading towards Britain – and with the smell of fresh loaves as Odette let them into the large, warm kitchen.

"I thought food was in short supply because of the war," said Pat suspiciously. "You seem to have tons of it here."

"I bake things for all the Nazi troops," said Odette. "It is good because I overhear them as they eat. But it is also bad because poor French folk are starving." She sighed as she got the tea going. "I smuggle out all the food I can."

"In her stomach, by the look of things," Bo muttered to Pat.

Soon Odette was passing round mugs of tea. McMoo took a big swig and smacked his lips. "Delicious!"

"Odette, have you heard anything about a British scientist called Sir Ivor Throbswitch being taken by the Nazis?" asked Pat.

She nodded. "Local soldiers say that a

British scientist is building a secret weapon in a lab disguised as a farmhouse. Some very important Nazis are flying here to see it."

"Old Ivor didn't waste much time, did he?" McMoo looked troubled. "Odette, where is Doctor Von Gonk? We must get him to Britain as soon as possible."

"I am holding him in this bakery," she revealed. "The escape plan has been worked out. Already he is well hidden in a crate of pies — and this very night, a lorry will arrive to drive him away to the nearest port."

"Ingenious!" McMoo gulped down the rest of his tea. "He can eat the pies on the journey to keep his strength up."

"Prof, I think I should take Doctor Von Gonk to old Churchill myself, to make sure nothing happens to him on the way," said Bo. "The Nazis mustn't get him back."

"That's a very good, very brave idea,"

said McMoo, and Pat nodded proudly. "Pat and I will stay here with Odette and try to find Sir Ivor."

"Very well," said Odette, bustling away. "I will prepare another crate of pies . . ."

"Just make sure they're vegetable pies and not steak!" Bo grimaced and lowered her voice. "I just hope we really *can* trust Madame LaBarmer. She looks so much like Bessie it's frightening."

Then, suddenly, Odette burst back into the kitchen – looking frightened herself.

"The lorry to take Doctor Von Gonk has arrived," she gabbled, "but a platoon of Nazi soldiers has followed it here!"

"Uh-oh," said McMoo. "They're bound to come into the bakery."

Pat gasped. "And if they find us . . . we're doomed!"

Chapter Five

THE FOREST OF FEAR

"No one panic," said McMoo urgently. "Here's what we do. Pat and I will create a distraction to lead the soldiers away. Odette, while we are gone you must hide Bo in the other crate and get her and Von Gonk onto the lorry." Bo opened her mouth to protest – but McMoo stuck a bun in it. "Don't argue – *mooo*ve. And good luck!"

Bo nodded reluctantly as Odette led her away.

"Er, what distraction did you have in mind, Professor?" asked Pat.

"We'll think of something," said McMoo. Grabbing a sack of crusty rolls, he led the way to the back door and Pat followed him outside.

As they made their way round to the front of the bakery, it wasn't just the cold night air that made Pat shiver. A big lorry was trundling down the road towards them. But a truck full of Nazi troops was overtaking it. Once the truck had passed, it stopped – blocking the lorry's way.

A tall, handsome Nazi soldier got out of the truck. He wore small round glasses and walked with a limp. "I am Colonel Vogel," he told the lorry driver in an icy voice. "What is your business here?"

The lorry driver shrugged. "The owner called me. She said I am to collect an urgent delivery."

"At three o'clock on a Sunday morning?" Vogel's eyes narrowed. "This sounds very suspicious . . ."

"It wasn't the owner who called you,

lorry driver," boomed McMoo, jumping out of hiding. "It was *us*, the Anti-Baking Brigade, luring you into a trap!"

Vogel swung round in surprise. "Halt!" he barked, and a dozen Nazi guns were suddenly pointing straight at McMoo. "Do not move!"

"Stop cruelty to pastry!" yelled McMoo. He started lobbing rolls at the Nazis. "Save dough from destruction!"

"Pies are evil! Bread is bad!" Pat added, throwing a few rolls himself. "Bagels are devilish!"

"And an anagram of bread is *beard*," roared McMoo. "Would you eat a beard? Ugh!"

Vogel dodged an especially crusty roll and turned to his men, who were already piling off the truck. "Stop these loonies!" he cried. "At once!"

"Come on, Pat – bun!" McMoo cried. "Er, I mean, *run!*"

And as Vogel and the soldiers came charging towards them, Pat sped away after the professor into the nearby woods.

In the moonlight it was hard to tell what was shadow and what was solid – until you ran into it. And Pat could hear the sound of Nazi boots crashing through the forest behind them. Twigs snapped underfoot with a sound like rifle shots. Then *real* rifle shots started up, twice as loud again. Bullets whizzed past Pat's head as he and McMoo ran deeper and deeper into the woods.

"Professor, they're catching us up," Pat panted. "What are we going to do?"

"Pull out your ringblender!" said McMoo, ducking into a clearing as more bullets zinged through the darkness. "And hide those human clothes. Now!"

As Pat yanked the metal ring from his nose, he understood the professor's plan. The Nazis were chasing after two crazy men – not a couple of stray bulls. So he put the ringblender in his pocket, wriggled out of his human clothes and chucked them into a bush. McMoo did the same, then the two of them stood behind a tree.

Most of the Nazis went crashing straight past. But Vogel's limp had slowed him down, and he paused in the clearing with one of his men.

"We will catch them, sir," said the soldier.

"You had better," Vogel warned him. "Even as we speak, that British fool Sir Ivor Throbswitch is finishing his new weapon at the farmhouse for tomorrow's demonstration. Many important observers are coming from Germany, and I do *not* want them pelted with bread by these anti-bakery buffoons!"

The soldier nodded quickly – then jumped as he spotted Pat and McMoo across the clearing. "Sir, look!"

"They are only wild bulls," said Vogel with a thin smile. "Excuse me, my friends — have you seen two men running by?"

Pat chomped some grass, and McMoo mooed innocently.

"Ha — talking to cows! A good joke, no?" Vogel chuckled. "Let's go . . ."

As Vogel and the soldier moved away, Pat and McMoo picked up their clothes.

"So, Sir Ivor's weapon will be tested tomorrow," said McMoo thoughtfully. "I wonder what it is?"

"Who knows?" said Pat. "I just hope Bo and Von Gonk get away OK."

"Hooves crossed," McMoo agreed. "Come on. Let's try to find our way back to the bakery."

"OK." Pat nodded. "I hope we aren't lost."

"I've got a brilliant sense of direction!" McMoo protested, striding away. "Of course we aren't lost. I *never* get lost!"

An hour later, McMoo was looking all around in bafflement. "You know what, Pat?" he said. "I think we're lost!"

Pat sighed and shook his aching hooves. "Oh, well. At least we haven't bumped into Colonel Vogel and his men again."

"Hey, what's that over there?" McMoo squinted into the distant shadows. "It looks like a little cottage or something." He put his nose ring back into position. "Get your gear back on, Pat! We'll ask for directions – and maybe a cup of tea!"

A few moments later, he was banging on the battered old door. No lights came on at the windows, and no one came to answer.

"It looks a bit old and grotty," Pat murmured. "Perhaps no one lives here any more."

McMoo winked at him. "In that case, let's pop in and rest for a while." He whacked the door above the lock extra hard, and it creaked open. "I'll go first."

He went inside, and Pat crept cautiously after him. The run-down old cottage had no electricity, so Pat found an oil lamp and some matches and McMoo lit it. Smoky, sputtering light filled the cottage's little living room.

Pat gasped. Tied up in the corner were two old men in long white coats with even longer white hair. One was tall and one was short. They tried to speak, but gags were tied tightly around their mouths. McMoo quickly pulled the gags away. "Are you all right?"

"Who are you?" demanded the short man in a posh English voice.

"I'm Pat and this is Professor McMoo," said Pat. "Who are you?"

"I am Sir Ivor Throbswitch," said the short man.

"And I am Doctor Herbert Von Gonk," said his taller companion in a German accent.

"The famous scientists?" McMoo stared at them. "No, you *can't* be."

"Of course you can't," Pat agreed. "Sir Ivor is preparing a weapon in a farmhouse and Doctor Von Gonk is in a crate on his way to England."

"Poppycock!" said Sir Ivor. "We have both been tied up in this hut for days."

"I only wish I *was* on my way to England," said Von Gonk sadly. "Not all Germans believe the Nazis are right. I was captured while trying to escape!"

"And now someone who *looks* like you is escaping instead," McMoo realized. "Odette is smuggling out an impostor – while a fake Sir Ivor works on a Nazi weapon!"

Pat gasped. "Then both the Nazis *and* the Resistance are being tricked!"

"*Enough*," came a roaring mechanical voice from behind them. "You have learned too much."

Pat and McMoo whirled round – to discover a large, sinister bull-like creature standing behind them. The creature wore sleek, shiny armour. Its horns were silver spikes. "T-23" was printed on its chest. Its baleful eyes glowed green – and the end of its nasty-looking gun was shining bright red.

"A t-t-t-ter-moo-nator!" stammered Pat.

"You have interfered with our plans for the last time, C.I.A. scum," said Ter-moo-nator T-23, raising its ray gun. "For you, the war is *over* . . ."

Chapter Six

ENCOWNTER AT SEA

"Duck, Pat!" McMoo shouted. The two C.I.A. agents dived aside as the ter-moo-nator opened fire. *ZZ-ZZAP!* A blast of red light spat from the ray gun and shattered the window behind them.

Pat grabbed a small table from the floor beside him and hurled it at T-23. At the same moment, McMoo jumped up and kicked the gun from the ter-moo-nator's hand. The weapon flew across the room – and conked Sir Ivor Throbswitch on the head. "Ow, that hurt," the old man complained.

"Sorry!" said McMoo. But while the professor was distracted, the raging

ter-moo-nator grabbed him by the
throat with one huge hoof and slammed
him against the wall. McMoo struggled
to free himself, gasping for air . . .

ZZ-ZZAP!

Suddenly, T-23's massive metal body
glowed red. His grip on McMoo grew
weaker and then he collapsed to the
ground.

"Got you!" cried Pat. He had scooped
up the fallen ray gun and now sat

clutching it tightly. "A direct hit!"

"Well done, Pat," croaked McMoo,
and the young bull glowed with pride.
"That ter-moo-nator was a real pain in
the neck!"

"Yes, good shooting," Sir Ivor added.
"That rotten robot-bull thing has had us
in his clutches for days."

"And he's got ever such cold hands,"
added Von Gonk with a shudder.
"Wherever did he come from?"

"He's certainly not from around here," said McMoo grimly. "What was he planning? Tell us all you know."

"He said he'd been in France for weeks," said Sir Ivor. "First he took over this abandoned cottage, and filled it with stacks and stacks of butter . . . then he and two more creatures like him turned an abandoned local farmhouse into a secret high-tech lab."

"Butter . . ." Pat frowned. "Professor, didn't Yak say the F.B.I. was stealing butter in its own time?"

McMoo nodded. "But what do those barking bulls need it for?"

"Shhh!" said Sir Ivor. "I don't know what you're on about, but someone's coming!"

Sure enough, Pat could hear the sound of heavy footsteps approaching . . .

"Professor, Pat!" Odette LaBarmer stood in the doorway. "I'm so glad you are all right. Vogel and his Nazis have given up their search for you. I came looking as soon as it was safe."

"I'm not sure 'safe' is the right word, Odette," said McMoo. "But look who we've found – Sir Ivor Throbswitch and—"

"Doctor Von Gonk?" Odette's face turned as white as a floury bap. "Impossible! I have just loaded you onto a lorry in a crate of pies!"

"I'm afraid you've sent a *fake* Von Gonk to England with Bo," said McMoo. "The question is, what is he planning to do when he gets there?"

"This is terrible!" Odette wailed.

Pat watched her suspiciously. She looked really upset, but was she only acting? "Odette, can we get Bo and Von Gonk off that lorry?"

"I fear not." Odette shook her head. "The port is not far from here. The crates will have been loaded onto a boat by now, ready to sneakily sail to England."

"Then let's get back to the bakery," said McMoo. "Odette, you must have a secret transmitter – we can use it to warn Churchill about that impostor."

"I *did* have one," said Odette, looking flustered. "But when I tried to use it to tell Mr Churchill that Von Gonk was on his way, I found it smashed. The impostor must have done it!"

Pat swapped a look with McMoo. Was Odette telling the truth – or did she simply not want them to warn Churchill that a fake was on his way? "Oh, Bo," he muttered miserably. "I do hope you're all right!"

Many miles away, in the cargo hold of a ship in the English Channel, Little Bo was chomping on a pie crust and feeling very fed up. The space Odette had left for her in the crate was big enough for a slender young lady, not a cow – so she was super-squashed up and aching all over.

Dr Von Gonk had been safely packed away before she'd arrived, but she hoped he was OK too. Odette had loaded them onto the lorry the moment the Nazis had run off after Pat and the professor. "You'd better be all right, boys," Bo breathed. "Or else!"

Suddenly, she heard the sound of wood splintering and a strange, clanking sound outside. It was coming closer . . . closer . . .

RRRIIIIPPP! The top was torn off her crate! She gasped to see two glowing green eyes glaring down at her.

There was a ter-moo-nator on board the ship!

"Blimey," said Bo in alarm, "where did you spring from?"

The robo-bull smoothed out his white lab coat and smiled. "Allow me to introduce myself. I am Ter-moo-nator T-60." He tapped the ringblender in his nose. "But the British will believe I am Doctor Von Gonk . . ."

"We'll see about *that*." Thinking fast, Bo pushed a pie into the ter-moo-nator's ugly face. Then she kicked her way out of her crate — and whacked the metal monster in the shins while she was at it.

T-60 gave a metallic snort of anger and lunged for her. Bo tried to duck aside, but she was just too slow. A cast-iron hoof swatted her to the floor, and her ringblender bounced away into the shadows. She gasped as the ter-moo-nator picked her up and strode from the cargo hold.

"Put me down, you stupid slab of techno-beef!" It was dark and cold out on the deck. T-60 was heading for the side of the ship, and Bo struggled furiously as she realized what he was up to. "I said, put me down!"

"Certainly," T-60 growled. And he threw her overboard with an almighty, freezing splash!

"No!" gasped Bo, struggling helplessly in the churning grey sea. The ter-moo-nator's gloating eyes were like green lanterns, fading into the night as the ship left Bo far behind . . .

Chapter Seven

THE SLIPPERY HORROR

Trying to keep calm, Bo stared around in the moonlit gloom. There was nothing to see but sea! For how long could she keep afloat? Her clothes were weighing her down, so she kicked them off.

"I'll just have to head back to shore," she decided. So Bo took a deep breath and started squirting milk from her udder to propel herself backwards in the choppy water, like a cow-shaped motorboat zooming through the night.

Several minutes passed. Waves broke over her head. The icy wetness chilled her to the bone. And then Bo felt her milk beginning to run dry!

"Oh, no," she groaned, and started doing the backstroke. She *had* to get to land!

Then, suddenly, with a thrill of hope, she saw the lights of another boat! Desperately she swam towards it, mooing like a foghorn to attract the sailors' attention. Since she had lost her ringblender and clothes, they would see her as an ordinary cow lost at sea. Bo wasn't sure many cows *were* lost at sea, but hopefully her novelty value would mean they would fish her out . . .

As she neared the boat, Bo saw fishermen on board – and a big Nazi symbol painted on the side. But she wasn't about to refuse a lift from anyone right now. Mooing weakly and fluttering her eyelids, Bo was relieved when the men on board spotted her and lowered a big net into the water to haul her up.

"Ta, fellas!" she mooed. But as she sat shivering in the net, surrounded by staring sailors speaking a language she couldn't understand, Bo knew her problems were far from over. How was she ever going to find Pat and the professor again?

The sun was still slowly rising as McMoo, Odette and Pat crept quietly through the French forest. They had left Sir Ivor Throbswitch and Dr Von Gonk safely at the bakery, and now they were heading for the farmhouse where the mysterious weapon would soon be tested.

"It is hard to believe this incredible story you have told me," said Odette. "Metal bulls? Evil impostors? And yet I feel in my heart it is true ..." She stopped them suddenly in their tracks. "The farmhouse is just the other side of these trees. But Colonel Vogel will have it well guarded."

"I'll check it out," said Pat, climbing a tree for a better look. As he popped his head out through the leafy branches, he saw a bunch of old farm buildings at one end of a very large field. Standing at the other end were a

Nazi tank, a field gun and a massive old-fashioned helicopter with two rotors. Pat recognized some of Vogel's men standing to attention outside the entrance.

"That's the place all right," he said, dropping back down. "And a couple of high branches should give us a great view of the action!"

Odette nodded. "While you two watch, I shall stand guard down here and check that no one sneaks up on us."

"Good thinking," said McMoo. "Come on, Pat! Give me a bunk-up . . ."

The two C.I.A. agents clambered up the tree and settled themselves to watch. Before long they could hear cars arriving, and Nazi officers and observers started to file into the field.

Then a ter-moo-nator came into view. He was wearing a white lab coat over a three-piece suit, and carried a

remote control in his hand.

"Odette!" hissed McMoo. "Pop up here for a moment."

A few seconds later, the leaves rustled and parted as Odette appeared. Her eyes widened. "Pastry above! That fellow in the white coat looks exactly like Sir Ivor Throbswitch!"

"Thanks, you can go again now," said McMoo, and Odette popped back down below.

"So while that ter-moo-nator's wearing his ringblender, humans see him as Sir Ivor," Pat muttered.

McMoo nodded. "That proves you were right, Pat. The F.B.I. is trying to trick both sides in this war."

"But why?" whispered Pat.

"Perhaps we'll soon find out," said McMoo. "Looks like that ter-moo-*faker* is ready to start his demonstration."

"Your attention please," said the ter-moo-nator, standing in the middle of the field. "You have come here today to witness the weapon that will win you the war. Behold . . . the *Butter-Bot!*"

The assembled Nazis looked puzzled. "What is this Butter-Bot?" one elderly general asked.

"See for yourself!" said the ter-moo-nator. He fiddled with his remote control and, suddenly, a loud slurping noise started up from within the farmhouse. The next moment, a giant, greasy yellow monster came stamping out from inside. Its enormous arms and legs were smooth and slippery, and a single eye blazed red in its blank face.

Pat gasped. "So *that's* where all the stolen butter's been going. The F.B.I. has

used it to build a secret weapon!"

"Of course!" McMoo groaned. "Butter is being rationed in *this* time, so they had to steal it from elsewhere."

The old general didn't look impressed. "This dairy concoction is supposed to win us the war? Absurd!"

The ter-moo-nator smiled. "The Butter-Bot is made of intelligent 'battle-butter', controlled by tiny computer chips. It is hundreds of years ahead of its time!"

"He's right there," muttered McMoo. "A weapon of the future, brought back to the past . . ."

"Butter cannot stand up to bullets and bombs," the general insisted. "You were kidnapped to make weapons for us – not to waste good food!"

The fake Sir Ivor glared at him. "Observe what happens when the Butter-Bot tangles with a tank!"

He gave a signal, and the tank

suddenly roared into life. Pat watched as it trundled towards the Butter-Bot. It fired an enormous explosive shell at the monster – *SPLOTT!* The butter sucked it up, then spat it back out at the tank. *BOOMMMM!* The tank went up in smoke, setting fire to a nearby tree.

Pat and McMoo swapped worried looks as the Nazi bigwigs gasped. "Amazing!" cried the general.

"The Butter-Bot can dowse flames with ease," said the ter-moo-nator. "Observe!"

The Butter-Bot hurled a huge yellow gobbet at the blazing tree – and extinguished the fire in a single sticky moment.

"Ooooh!" said the audience.

"And now, the Butter-Bot will deal with a field gun," the ter-moo-nator went on, flicking switches on his remote.

Colonel Vogel was manning the cannon-like field gun with two soldiers.

They got ready to fire – but already the Butter-Bot was squelching towards them. Suddenly, it stretched out its arms into enormous snaking streams of butter and slooshed all the men away. They skidded about on the grass in buttery confusion.

"Note how the Butter-Bot can also turn itself rock hard – like butter kept in the fridge – to squash enemy equipment," said the smug ter-moo-nator.

The next moment, the monster's huge eye narrowed and it stamped the field gun into pieces.

The Nazi onlookers clapped and cheered. Even Vogel shouted "Bravo!" although he was still too slippery to stand up again.

But McMoo and Pat both wore deep frowns on their faces.

"With a few hundred weapons like that, the Nazis could win the war," McMoo murmured.

"But the F.B.I. will be using its fake Von Gonk to make weapons for Britain too," Pat reminded him. "Whatever are those bolshy bulls up to?"

"McMoo! Pat!" Odette called urgently from the foot of the tree. "Come down here — quickly!"

Pat gulped. It sounded like something bad had happened. He and McMoo swiftly scrambled down the tree.

Only to find Ter-moo-nator T-23

waiting for them with a ray gun! He wore the fake uniform of a Nazi major-general and a ringblender through his nose . . . and Odette LaBarmer stood smiling beside him. The two C.I.A. agents stared in shock and disbelief.

"Bo and I were right from the start," Pat wailed. "You're as rotten as your relatives!"

"Churchill trusted you so I thought I could too . . ." McMoo shook his head. "How could I have been so wrong? I mean, *me*, wrong? That just doesn't happen!"

"Enough." Odette stuffed a bun into his mouth. "I told you they would be here, Major-General. Two British spies!"

"Oh, they are far more than simple spies," hissed T-23, stepping towards them. "And soon they shall be dealt with *for ever*!"

Chapter Eight

THE F.B.I. MASTER PLAN

Back on the fishing boat, Bo was so exhausted that she finally fell asleep. But she woke up quickly when she heard a babble of angry cries in German. She blinked blearily, trying to work out why everyone was shouting and waving big meat cleavers in her direction.

Then she realized: she had dozed off lying on her back, revealing her udder to the world. An udder that was still painted with a Union Jack! The colours had run a bit after her struggle in the sea, but the pattern was still clearly visible.

"Flip," said Bo as the angry fishermen

drew closer. "That'll teach me to use marker pens!" (But of course, to the fishermen, her words came out as "Mooo-ooo".)

"Bad cow!" hissed a Nazi fisherman in a woolly hat and halting English. "You fall off British boat, yes? Well, that will make you taste all the better!"

Bo saw how hungry the fishermen looked, and remembered Professor McMoo telling her that food was in short supply during the war. No wonder they had rescued her – they were going to turn her into a dozen dinners!

Glancing round, Bo could see that land was in sight. They were nearing a harbour. "Time I was off!" she yelled – and she somersaulted backwards over the side of the ship and into the sea. A few squirts from her recovering udder had her racing through the shallow waves towards the shore.

But already people at the harbour were

shaking their fists at her angrily, alerted by the fishermen. She wasn't sure what they were saying but guessed it was something like, "*Stop, enemy cow! Get in our stomachs!*" And even as she splashed out of the sea and onto the sand, they were charging down to get her . . .

"I shall fight on the beaches!" cried Bo. She whacked one man with her hooves, and blasted another in the face with a sudden stream of milk. Both of them went down, stunned. But many

others were coming to take their places. "Not fair," she groaned. "How am I going to get out of this?"

Then Bo noticed something nearby in the harbour – and smiled. Perhaps there *was* an escape route after all . . .

Escape was high on Pat's mind too. But as T-23 marched him and McMoo past Nazi guards into the secret farmhouse base, he couldn't imagine how they would ever get out again. Pat looked up at the giant Butter-Bot as it shot blasts of yellow goo at the helicopter circling overhead, and shuddered at its sheer pasteurized power.

T-23 had sent Odette away almost at once. "You will wait at your bakery and lock up the real Sir Ivor and Von Gonk," he'd said. "I will send guards to collect them later."

"Yes, sir." Odette had saluted and lumbered away.

"We really should have known." Pat sighed. "Never trust a Barmer, no matter how nice she seems."

T-23 marched them into a wooden outbuilding full of rusting farm machinery. "At last," he growled. "I have captured our greatest enemies!"

"What are you up to here in 1940?" said McMoo coldly.

"Can't you guess, my oh-so-clever professor?" sneered T-23. "The fake Von Gonk is another ter-moo-nator. Very soon now he shall demonstrate an identical Butter-Bot to the rulers of Britain. Like the Nazis, they will think it is the perfect weapon that can win them the war."

McMoo frowned. "So each side will make hundreds of Butter-Bots – unaware that the other side are doing exactly the same."

T-23 smiled. "And when the rulers of Britain and Germany come to inspect their finished army of Butter-Bots they will find they no longer work – because *we* will override the controls!" He produced something that looked like a yellow mobile phone. "This device will make the Butter-Bots turn on their creators – and squish them. Then we shall declare war on *all* humans, whichever side they are on! Without their leaders, the people will panic. They will be no match for the slippery might of our creamy-churned warriors!"

McMoo scowled. "And once you've conquered the British and the Nazis, you can build more Butter-Bots and attack their allies."

"Precisely," said T-23. "America . . . Russia . . . Italy . . . Japan . . . All shall fall before the power of the F.B.I.!"

"You'll have to steal an awful lot of butter," said Pat.

T-23 shook his metal head. "We shall force all 1940s cows to make vats of butter just for us — to aid our war effort."

McMoo stared. "That's horrible!"

"We shall teach all cows to hate and to fight," said the ter-moo-nator. "We shall make cows strong — turn them into lethal moo-niacs who will conquer the world. World War Two shall become World War *Moo*. And you, McMoo, shall use your brainpower to help it happen . . . or *die*!"

Chapter Nine

FURY IN THE FARMYARD

Pat and McMoo looked at each other helplessly as T-23 rubbed his metal hooves together with glee. "I will give you a short while to decide, Professor," the ter-moo-nator said. "I wish to watch the end of the Butter-Bot demonstration. But then I shall return . . ."

"Don't hurry back," called McMoo, as T-23 went out and locked the door behind him. Then the professor sighed. "Well, Pat, we're in a pickle and a half this time."

Pat nodded. "What we need right now is a miracle."

Then, not quite on cue – about three and a half minutes later, in fact – he heard someone unlock the door. It swung open again . . . to reveal Odette LaBarmer!

"I said we needed a miracle, not a big fat traitor," Pat grumbled. "What are you doing here? Come to gloat?"

"No," she replied with a smile. "I have come to set you free!"

"Eh?" McMoo frowned. "Did I miss a bit?"

"You were the one who got us captured in the first place!" Pat protested.

"I am sorry about that." Odette bowed her head. "That Nazi in the woods sneaked up on me. I had to convince him I was on his side or he would have arrested me – or worse! And that would leave Sir Ivor and Doctor Von Gonk helpless at my bakery."

Pat raised his eyebrows. "So you only pretended to betray us?"

"Of course!" Odette declared. "It is our duty to destroy that buttery monster. Now, all three of us are inside the Nazis' secret base – exactly where we need to be!"

"Odette, you sneaky thing!" McMoo grinned. "But how did you get past the guards on the gate?"

She shrugged. "I gave them a drugged pie and snatched their keys when they fell asleep. Now, please, we must hurry!"

Odette led them outside. They could hear shouts and yells and machine guns firing.

"Sounds like the Butter-Bot is still being put through its paces," said Pat.

They peeped round a haystack and found Colonel Vogel's men finally getting up from their big sticky puddle. The field gun was just a mangled piece of metal, the tank was lying in pieces beneath the half-burned tree and the helicopter was covered in goo. The one-eyed Butter-Bot stared round as if seeking out fresh enemies, while the gathered Nazis clapped and cheered. T-23 and the fake Sir Ivor smiled knowingly at each other.

"We must get the override device that T-23 showed us," McMoo murmured. "It's our only way to get full control of that thing."

"Then what are we waiting for?" said Odette. She hitched up one trouser leg to reveal a number of long sausage rolls tucked down her sock. "It is time to attack!"

With that, Odette hurled her sausage rolls with deadly accuracy. One of them caught the elderly general under the chin. He gasped and fell. As the nearest Nazis tried to help him up, more savoury missiles found their uniformed targets and knocked them to the ground.

"What is happening?" T-23 swung round and saw them — and his eyes glowed even greener with anger. "Intruder alert. Unleash the Butter-Bot!"

The fake Sir Ivor reached for his remote. "Oh no you don't!" cried Pat, lowering his head to charge. *CLANNG!* Horns clashed against metal as Pat butted him in the bottom. Bright blue sparks burst from the fake scientist's bum and he went crashing to the ground. At the same time McMoo galloped over

quickly, shoved T-23 aside and stamped the remote control into the mud.

At once, the Butter-Bot jerked about, clutching its big, buttery head. T-23 pulled out his override device to get the weapon back under control. But Odette moved faster. She threw a doughnut with ninja-like skill and knocked the gadget from his grip. T-23 warbled with rage – but then the blundering Butter-Bot shut him up by stepping on him!

McMoo grabbed the override and hit a red button, and the Butter-Bot squelched to a squidgy standstill.

Vogel pointed at Pat and McMoo. "It's the Anti-Baking Brigade," he shouted. "They've even got the baker on their side! Men, *get them*!"

Suddenly, two soldiers came charging at Pat from different directions. "Pulsating potatoes!" he cried in alarm. At the last moment he ducked down, and the Nazis collided with an *OOOF!*

Pulling a croissant from her shoe, Odette used it as a boomerang and knocked out another two soldiers with a single throw.

But that still left Vogel and six more fighting men. Professor McMoo stared at them . . .

And then he ran away!

"Professor!" Pat cried, shocked to his hooves. "Come back! You can't leave us!"

"Don't interrupt me when I'm

working out my speed and angle of approach, Pat!" said McMoo.

And Pat realized that the professor was running with his head twisted to one side – right at the burned, butter-drenched tree. *THWACK!* McMoo smashed the tree down – and the trunk was left speared on the end of his horns! He straightened his head so the trunk was horizontal. For a moment, he struggled to hold it up, like a weightlifter lifting a heavy barbell. Then, with a snort of effort, he charged back towards the startled Nazis.

THUNK!
"ARRGH!"
SPLASH!

McMoo smashed through Vogel and his soldiers and sent them flying into a big trough of sheep dip! They splashed around in a daze, while the crowd of Nazi bigwigs ran for their lives in a hail of Odette's rock cakes.

Pat rushed over to tug the tree trunk from McMoo's horns. "That was amazing!"

"Just a simple matter of applied force and speed equations – any mega-brilliant genius could have done the same!" said McMoo modestly. He pulled out the yellow override device. "Now, let's get rid of this thing . . ."

He fiddled with the controls, and the Butter-Bot began to bubble and melt. Its single big eye flopped out of its unfeeling face and hit the ground with a splat. The rest of it soon followed as it dissolved into greasy gunge.

"There!" McMoo clapped happily. "Nothing left but a sticky puddle of microchips!"

"Er, that's really cool, Professor," said Pat nervously. "But now there's nothing holding down T-23!"

Sure enough, the butter-drenched ter-moo-nator leader rose up from a small crater in the field. He was shaking with fury – and his ray gun was aimed right at them. "You shall pay for this!" he snarled.

"Pay for a lot of stolen butter?" McMoo snorted. "Not likely!"

T-23's metal fingers tightened on the trigger . . .

Chapter Ten

TERROR IN THE SKY

Pat grabbed the professor's hoof and closed his eyes as T-23 prepared to fire. *Bye-bye, Bo*, he thought, hoping his sister was still OK.

But suddenly, the sharp roar of an engine tore through the air. Pat's eyes snapped open to see a funny-looking aeroplane zooming down from the sky. It seemed to have two enormous skis stuck underneath it – and it was heading straight for them! Or rather, straight for T-23 . . .

"Down, everyone!" boomed McMoo.

Pat, McMoo and Odette dived for cover. The ter-moo-nator leader turned in surprise — and one of the skis clonked him under the chin. He was sent flying through the air with an electronic squawk and smashed into the tree stump.

Pat blinked in amazement. "Where did that thing come from?"

"It's an amphibious aircraft," McMoo enthused. "Just look at it! It has wheels hidden in those floats underneath so it can land on the ground or on water."

"Never mind the plane, boys," said Odette, pointing in amazement as the aircraft landed bumpily in the field. "Look who's driving – it's a . . . *cow*!"

Pat's eyes grew wide as he grinned in astounded delight. "Bo!"

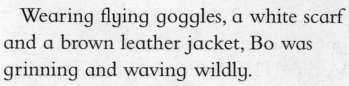

Wearing flying goggles, a white scarf and a brown leather jacket, Bo was grinning and waving wildly.

"She must have lost her ringblender," said McMoo. "But that's easily fixed!" He ran over to where T-23 lay sprawled beneath the tree and plucked out the ring from the robo-bull's metal nose. Then he quickly tossed it to Bo as she jumped out of the aeroplane.

Odette pointed in horror at T-23. "Great rolls of heaven!" she cried. "That major-general has turned into one of those metal bulls you spoke of! But how?"

"We'll explain later," Pat told her. "But look, at least that flying cow has gone — and Bo's here in her place!"

"Little bruv! Prof!" Bo grabbed them both in her tightest hug. "I see you can't get by without me — as usual!"

"But how did you get here?" asked McMoo happily.

"I was being chased by hundreds of hungry humans around the harbour," she said. "Then I saw this plane floating in the water, so I borrowed it."

"You mean you could actually fly it?" said Pat.

"It's easy," Bo declared. "I only knocked the roofs off a couple of houses on the way! I was looking for the bakery, and I accidentally flew over this field. Lucky for you that I did!"

McMoo nodded. "But why aren't you

in England? Did you run into trouble with that fake Von Gonk?"

"You bet I did – he chucked me overboard!" Bo frowned. "But how did you know he was a fake?"

"It's a long story," said Pat. And while Odette stood there, still scratching her head in amazement, he told it to Bo.

"Now we must fly to Britain at once and warn Churchill in person," declared McMoo.

Odette frowned. "In a Nazi plane? The British will shoot us down!"

"We have to try," said McMoo, holding up the yellow override device. "At least while we have this, we can take control of the British Butter-Bot before it can cause too much trouble!"

ZZAPP! Suddenly, McMoo gasped as the device was blasted from his hoof and destroyed by a red ray of light.

Pat pointed. "It's T-23!"

"You will never triumph, McMoo!"

growled the ter-moo-nator leader, waving his gun.

Another bolt of deadly light whizzed past Pat's head. He turned to find that the fake Sir Ivor had recovered – and was also pointing a gun at them.

"Run for the plane!" McMoo shouted.

They fled, dodging death rays every step of the way. "Without the override, how will we deal with the other Butter-Bot?" panted Pat.

"I'll think of something," said McMoo. "Odette, can you fly a helicopter?"

"I have a hunch I'm going to find out!" she replied, puffing for breath.

McMoo pointed to the buttery 'copter in the corner of the field. "Take that one and fly back to your bakery."

"I shall try," she declared bravely. "How hard can it be? I'll just use my loaf!"

"Good luck," said McMoo. "I'll signal you once we're in the air!"

They reached Bo's borrowed plane. She scrambled into the pilot's seat and McMoo and Pat piled in behind her. Both ter-moo-nators fired at Odette as she lumbered on towards the helicopter – but all they managed to hit was her baker's hat.

"Get us up, Bo!" McMoo shouted.

"I'm on the case!" Bo replied. The plane took off jerkily, rocking as ray blasts slammed into its sides. But luckily it held together as they soared away noisily into the sky.

"Ya-hoooo!" whooped Pat.

A few moments later, Odette's helicopter wobbled into view alongside them as they flew over the forest.

McMoo grabbed the pilot's radio and spoke into it. "Good work, Odette. But our foes will soon follow us."

Odette's voice crackled back to him. "What can we do?"

"I have a plan," said McMoo, smiling craftily. "But it all depends on *you* . . ."

Soon, Bo was flying the aircraft at 18,000 feet over the English Channel. McMoo sat beside her in the cockpit, with Pat just behind. It was small and cramped, a metal shell with more buttons and switches than the Time Shed. The rumble of the engine and the whoosh of the wind outside made it very noisy. But, with a thrill of nerves,

Pat forgot all that as land came into sight.

"So here we are, flying a Nazi plane in broad daylight, heading for London," said Bo sourly. "We might as well hold up a big sign saying, *Shoot us down, please!*"

"I only hope Odette makes it through in her helicopter," said McMoo. "My plan won't work without her."

Pat sighed. It was a pretty wild plan even by the professor's standards. He knew it might not work even if Odette *did* make it through.

"Mind out of the way, Pat," said Bo, squinting into her rear-view mirror. "Someone's coming up behind us. Is that Odette?"

McMoo looked for himself. "No," he
said gravely. "It's a Nazi fighter plane,
and it looks like it's going to attack!"
Suddenly, the rattle of guns pounded out
over the roar of the engine, and McMoo
groaned. "You know, every now and
then, I wish I could be wrong for once!"

"So do I," said Bo, banking sharply to
the right to avoid the gunfire. "Hang on!"

As they swooped crazily through the
sky, Pat glimpsed a flash of steel and
four glowing eyes in the cockpit of the

enemy plane. "The ter-moo-nators!" he
cried, transfixed with fear. "They must
have had a plane hidden at the
farmhouse."

"I'll see if I can lose them!" Bo yanked
back hard on the control stick. Pat's
stomach lurched as the plane performed
a steep climbing turn to the left. Bullets
zinged through the blue sky around
them.

"Hang on," warned Bo. "Looks like
more planes up ahead."

Pat saw them – a squadron of seven, painted shades of green in camouflage patterns with a big target on the side. "They're Hurricanes, aren't they, Professor? Like the one we saw at the air show."

"Only these planes will be firing real bullets," said McMoo. "And they think we are the enemy!"

"Caught between the British and the Nazis," cried Bo as Hurricane bullets zipped through the air in fierce flashes. "We haven't got a chance!"

Chapter Eleven

SHOT DOWN FOR THE SHOWDOWN

Bo pushed forward on the control stick. "I'll try to cut underneath them and get on their tails," she bellowed. "They can't shoot us if we're behind them!"

The plane plunged into a spin. "Whoaaaaa!" wailed Pat.

"I definitely prefer travel by Time Shed!" McMoo agreed.

By now, England was green and bright below them. Bo sent the plane climbing up again in a tight circle. Pat saw five of the Hurricanes bank away from them.

"Hey, most of the Hurricanes are

attacking the ter-moo-nators' plane!"
said Bo.

"It's got bigger guns," shouted McMoo
over the scream of the engine. "It's more
of a threat than we are."

"But there are still three planes after
us!" Pat yelled. More bullets pinged past
the cockpit as the nearest Hurricane
dived towards them.

"They're aiming for our engines to
bring us down," McMoo cried. "And
we're still a good ten minutes away
from London!"

But suddenly, the attacking Hurricane
dropped away with black smoke
pouring from its side. The pilot ejected
and soon had his parachute open.

"Luckily for us, T-23 is a rubbish
shot," said McMoo grimly. "He tried to
get us but he hit the Hurricane!"

"If we can just hold out a little
longer," said Pat desperately.

"I'm working on it," Bo assured him.

"But what am I supposed to do when we reach the secret base? Land on the roof?"

"Oh, dear." McMoo looked shifty. "I was so busy worrying about getting here, I forgot to worry about landing!"

Suddenly, a shadow fell over them. "Oh, no!" cried Pat. "Hurricane right above us!"

"And another close behind," McMoo realized. Their plane shook as bullets pumped into its body. A flap of metal burst away from the side like a big black bird launching into flight. "That was our engine cover!"

The roar of the plane's motors soon sounded sickly. "We're losing speed!" Bo groaned as the plane started to dip. "I think we're going to crash!"

"We're not far from the secret base now." McMoo pointed down at a grey ribbon of water. "That's the river Thames. Try to crash there away from any of the boats so no one will get hurt."

"No one?" Bo gulped. "What about us?"

The engines were screaming as the plane spiralled down towards the river. Pat's stomach kept flipping like a pancake. "We'd better get ready to use our parachutes," he said.

"Everyone ready?" demanded McMoo. Pat and Bo nodded. "Eject!"

BANG! The plexiglass cover of the cockpit burst away and Pat found himself falling upwards! He pulled on the ripcord and the parachute opened with a whoosh of white canvas.

Then – *KA-SPLOOOSH!* The aircraft splashed down in the murky water of the Thames and a huge plume of spray rose up like a fountain. Several boats nearby were drenched but no one was hurt. Pat breathed a sigh of relief as he, Bo and McMoo floated down

over the roads beside the riverbank.

"We made it!" cheered Bo.

"But look," said Pat suddenly, staring down. Dozens of soldiers and air-raid wardens and even ordinary people were gathering below, pointing and shouting and waving any weapons they could lay their hands on. "That mob think we are Nazis trying to invade. They're going to get us!"

The C.I.A. agents landed with a bump in a busy street. Cars screeched to a halt, honking their horns. The angry crowd surged towards them, led by the soldiers. Pat covered his eyes and waited for the worst to happen . . .

But then he heard a familiar voice: "It's all right, everyone. They aren't Nazis, even if they were in a Nazi plane. They are friends of Winston Churchill himself!"

Pat opened his eyes. "Captain Walker!"

"Yay!" Bo ran over and gave the soldier a big kiss on the cheek. "Are we ever glad to see you!"

"I'm glad you're all back in one piece," said Walker, blushing. "But I'm surprised you let Doctor Von Gonk travel by himself. Did something go wrong?"

Bo nodded. "Just about everything!"

"I thought so," Walker continued.

"I opened every other crate, but each one was stuffed full of butter – and Von Gonk insisted on taking the whole lot to the secret base with him!"

"Uh-oh," said Pat. "Brand-new Butter-Bot, here we come!"

"Walker, the man you think is Von Gonk is an impostor," said McMoo breathlessly. "He must be stopped!"

Walker stared. "Are you sure?"

"Duh!" yelled Bo. "That's why we whizzed back to warn you!"

"We must tell Mr Churchill quickly," said McMoo. "Where is he?"

"He's at the base," said Walker, pale-faced. "Watching the demonstration of Von Gonk's amazing new weapon. We'd better find him right away!"

"First, you must tell the Royal Air Force not to attack a Nazi helicopter that's on its way here," McMoo told him. "It's vital – Sir Ivor Throbswitch and the real Doctor Von Gonk are on board with Odette LaBarmer."

"Well, strike me pink and call me a kipper!" said Walker, scratching his head as he turned to one of his men. "Sergeant Smith, take care of it."

"Yes, sir," said Smith, hurrying off to obey.

"Professor," hissed Pat, "what about T-23 and his metal mate?"

"Looks like the air force has already got them well under control," said McMoo, pointing upwards.

The Hurricanes had all ganged up on the Nazi plane, circling it tightly and forcing it into a nose-dive. Two metallic figures ejected as the plane made another safe but noisy splashdown in the Thames. As the waters foamed and bubbled over the sunken craft, T-23 and the fake Sir Ivor parachuted slowly through the air, ready to land a few streets away. The angry crowd dashed off to confront the new arrivals, and the soldiers went with them.

"My men will take care of that parachuting pair and bring them in double-quick," said Walker. "Now, come on!"

He led the way to the secret base beneath the building on the busy street. Soon, Pat, Bo and McMoo were following him down the stairs to the secret weapons-testing centre in the heart of the building. Waving aside a gaggle of guards, Walker opened the doors and crept into the enormous chamber beyond . . .

Pat grimaced, and Bo gasped. There was an identical Butter-Bot rampaging in the middle of the vast chamber. It was in "fridge-hard" mode, crushing an armoured car like a human would crush an old tin can. Churchill and a small group of British bigwigs were watching with excitement as the fake Von Gonk –

in reality a ter-moo-nator – twisted the
buttons on his remote control.

"He's the same one who chucked me
off the boat," Bo whispered to Pat. "His
name's T-60!"

"Thank you, Von Gonk," said Churchill gravely as the Butter-Bot stopped still. "This is a fine weapon—"

"Stop the test!" shouted McMoo, charging across the room between the Butter-Bot's enormous legs, with Pat and Bo close behind him. "That is not the real Von Gonk, and this weapon will destroy us all. It's all a trick!"

Churchill rose sternly from his seat. His observers whispered among themselves in confusion.

"Von Gonk" himself – Ter-moo-nator T-60 – spun round to face the professor. "It is you," he growled.

"True," said McMoo. "But it *isn't you*!"

So saying, he swiped T-60's ringblender. Churchill gasped, and the bigwigs yelped as the robo-bull was revealed.

"I don't believe it!" cried Churchill, his face going dark with fury. "Von Gonk was a metal monster all along!"

Bo tried to grab T-60's remote control but he kicked her aside and she fell into McMoo. Pat lunged forward to grab the device himself . . .

But suddenly, huge sticky fingers closed around his body. The Butter-Bot had grabbed him!

T-60 laughed and twisted a dial on the remote. "You wanted to stop my demonstration," he jeered. "Now you will become part of it!"

Pat gasped and struggled as he was lifted helplessly high up into the air. The Butter-Bot's huge red eye glared down at him as its creamy yellow fingers started to squeeze . . .

Chapter Twelve

THE FINAL, BUTTERY BATTLE

Pat struggled for breath as the Butter-Bot's grip grew tighter and tighter. He saw the onlookers down below staring in horror. But what had happened to Mr Churchill . . . ?

Then McMoo's voice rang commandingly across the hall. "Don't bother with small-fry, T-60!" he boomed. "Your plan may have failed, but you can still capture this country's leader. While you're wasting time, he's getting away!"

Pat frowned – then saw what he meant. Bo was dragging Churchill by his sleeve out of the testing room . . .

The next moment, Pat found himself slung to the floor like a sack of spuds. "Oof!" he gasped.

The Butter-Bot picked up T-60 instead. "McMoo is right," the ter-moo-nator snarled, fiddling with the remote. "The rest of you can wait — but Churchill must be mine. After him, my Butter-Bot!"

The buttery monster clomped away, covering the length of the enormous room in three mighty strides. McMoo helped Pat up and dusted him down.

"You fool, McMoo," said Captain Walker crossly. "Thanks to you, Mr Churchill is in direct danger!"

"It's all part of my plan, Walker," said McMoo, hopping about with excitement. "Bo is using Churchill to lure that monster outside — but everything depends on Odette arriving in time." He charged off after the Butter-Bot. "Come on, then!"

Pat and Walker followed him, hurtling up the steps four at a time and trying not to slip on the creature's buttery footprints. By the time they got upstairs to ground level, the Butter-Bot was surging out into the street beyond.

Pat burst through the doors after the professor and Walker. Turning to the left, he stared in horror. Sergeant Smith and his men were marching T-23 and the fake Sir Ivor down the crowded street. But the Butter-Bot bore down on the soldiers and flicked them away, before scooping up the two F.B.I. agents in its free hand.

People ran for their lives.

"Ha!" T-23 stared down at McMoo from his buttery vantage point. "Once we have captured Churchill we shall squish you all!"

Pat turned to his right and saw Bo scattering people in all directions, carrying the British leader away in a fireman's lift. She was running at an incredible speed, but the Butter-Bot was already looming up behind.

"Come on," muttered McMoo, staring frantically up at the sky. "Come on, come on, come on ..."

Then, suddenly, a huge helicopter zoomed overhead, escorted by a couple of Hurricanes. The Nazi symbols on the 'copter's side had been painted over with red, white and blue stripes and a funny red cross in the middle – the flag of the Free French.

McMoo punched the air. "*Yes!*"

The Hurricanes flew away and left the helicopter hovering above the street. The crowds of panicking people stopped running and stared up in amazement. So did Bo and Churchill. Even the Butter-Bot paused while its F.B.I. masters checked out this new arrival.

Then the helicopter doors opened to reveal Odette LaBarmer at the controls – and the real Sir Ivor Throbswitch and Dr Von Gonk behind her! They started to drop hundreds of thin brown squares down into the street below.

"People of London, don't be afraid!" McMoo bellowed. "That's *bread* falling from the sky. I know it's normally rationed, but today it's all free. Loads and loads of fresh *free* bread!"

An old woman picked up a couple of slices and licked her lips. "He's right!"

"Yes!" A man started dancing a little jig. "It's raining bread!"

McMoo stabbed a hoof at the Butter-Bot. "And *that* thing is made of solid butter," he yelled. "Look! It's trying to squish your brave prime minister. And only *you* can stop it. Because bread is butter's natural enemy – and those nice people up there are giving you enough to mop up every last blob of it."

"Go on, my friends," called Churchill, encouraging the crowd. "Tuck in!"

The bread kept on tumbling down from the helicopter. Hundreds of slices were already sticking to the Butter-Bot's body.

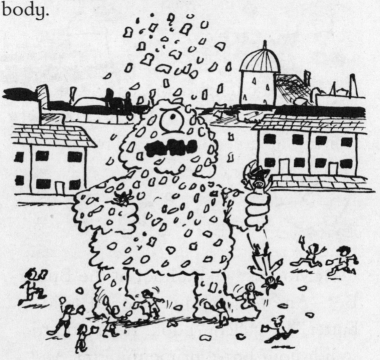

"Stay back," T-23 warned the gathering crowds.

But one little boy scooped up some of the Butter-Bot's foot with a crusty slice. "Delicious!" he said. "I haven't had as much butter as that in a fortnight!"

And suddenly, everyone charged *towards* the Butter-Bot!

"Attack!" cried T-60, pressing buttons on his remote. The Butter-Bot lifted one foot to crush the crowd, but it was too slow — already a flurry of fingers were clawing huge lumps from its sole and guzzling them down with tasty chunks of bread. The people's food had been rationed for nine months — and here was the biggest free meal they had ever seen!

"Hang on," yelled Sir Ivor. "We've got some French toast here somewhere too!"

Word spread even faster than the butter, and men, women and especially children came pouring in from other streets all around. The Butter-Bot was being whittled away. People were clambering all over it like ants on an ant hill. Even "fridge-hard" it could no longer defend itself — not while it held the ter-moo-nators in its buttery fists. And it wasn't long before T-23 and his

ter-moo-nator friends were wrenched
away from safety by hungry hands and
half trampled by the mob.

"Curse you, McMoo!" squawked T-23.
He pulled a flat silver time-travel
machine from underneath his chest-
plate and stood on it with his fellow
ter-moo-nators. "Our plans have failed,"
he growled. "Mission abort! Recall!
Mission aborrrrt!"

The three robo-bulls faded away in a cloud of black smoke. But the hungry crowd, busy scoffing the last sticky traces of the Butter-Bot, never noticed a thing.

"The F.B.I. has given up!" Pat cheered. "They've gone back to their own time."

Bo appeared, carrying Winston Churchill on her shoulders and smiling. "Blimey, Professor. Your plan actually worked!"

"So it has!" McMoo grinned. "Believe me, Bo – no one is more surprised than *I* am!"

Odette LaBarmer's helicopter landed on the roof high above the underground base. Pat, Bo and McMoo were waiting with Captain Walker and Churchill. As Odette wearily flopped out of the 'copter, McMoo grabbed her in a hug. Pat and Bo helped Sir Ivor and Dr Von Gonk down so that Churchill could shake their hands. In the street far

below, the people were still cheering and celebrating their good fortune.

"Professor," Pat asked quietly, "what about all those tiny computer chips they've eaten with the butter?"

"Perfectly harmless in the 1940s," McMoo assured him. "But if it happened in the 1980s, they would switch TV channels every time they burped!"

Churchill greeted Odette warmly. "You are a very brave woman, my dear," he told her. "You have fought not only Nazis, but monsters both sticky and mechanical. Will you rest with us in Britain for a while?"

"I cannot, sir," Odette told him in halting English. "Not until the people of France are free." She frowned. "Also, I think I left the oven on!"

Churchill smiled. "We shall smuggle you back to your bakery with much flour and yeast to make up for all you have used this glorious day." He turned to Sir Ivor and Von Gonk. "And you, gentlemen – will you stay?"

Sir Ivor nodded. "We want to work together to make the world a better place for everybody, wherever they are."

"And so we shall no longer make weapons for anyone," said Von Gonk firmly. "Instead, we shall work on better ways to heal the wounded on both sides."

A smile settled on Churchill's craggy features. "Gentlemen, I fear we shall not know peace for many years. But when it comes, fine people like you shall ensure it is a lasting one."

"Hear, hear to that!" said McMoo, slipping quietly away with Pat and Bo. "And now I think we'd better be getting back to the Time Shed. We've polished off the F.B.I.'s plans . . . let's do the same to a bucket of tea!"

★

In daylight it was much easier to climb up to where the Time Shed stood teetering on the bombsite.

Bo looked sadly around at the wreckage. "What a mess."

McMoo nodded. "But every day, both here and afar, heroes on all sides are working to make things better."

Bo nodded, and smiled back. "You know, I still can't believe that Bessie Barmer actually has a nice relative!"

Pat nodded. "I bet Odette's the only good Barmer since time began."

"I suppose even the nastiest person can find goodness inside if they look hard enough," said McMoo thoughtfully. "It just goes to show we should always keep an open mind. Because when people believe they are right no matter what . . . *that's* when wars can start." He gave his friends a big smile. "Right! Let's get off home, shall we?"

But as he unlocked the door and led the way inside, a bleeping sound started up. "Hey, it's the C.I.A. hotline!" said McMoo. Bo rushed inside and flicked a switch. Yak's face appeared on the monitor screen hanging from the rafters.

"Well done, team," Yak said, smiling. "You've smashed the F.B.I.'s sneakiest time-crime yet, and the butter robberies in our own age have stopped." He paused and smiled. "As Churchill once said, 'Never was so much owed by so many to so few.'"

"All you owe *us* is a few of those extra-tasty future tea bags," said McMoo with a grin. And even as he spoke, a small pile of them appeared at his feet. "Brilliant!"

"I'll brew up right away!" Pat offered.

Yak smiled. "Till next time, troops," he said as his face faded away. "The F.B.I. will be back to cause more trouble soon, without a doubt."

"Good!" McMoo declared. He curled his tail around the take-off lever and smiled at his two friends. "Because today we've proved that going on incredible missions for the C.I.A. really is our *bread and butter* — no matter *what* time it is!"

THE END

IT'S 'UDDER' MADNESS!

Genius cow Professor McMoo and his trusty sidekicks, Pat and Bo, are star agents of the C.I.A. – short for COWS IN ACTION! They travel through time, fighting evil bulls from the future and keeping history on the right track ...

When Professor McMoo invents a brilliant TIME MACHINE, he and his friends are soon attacked by a terrifying TER-MOO-NATOR — a deadly robo-cow who wants to mess with the past and change the future! And that's only the start of an incredible ADVENTURE that takes McMoo, Pat and Bo from a cow paradise in the future to the SCARY dungeons of King Henry VIII ...

It's time for action.